CODE OF THE
KRILLITANES

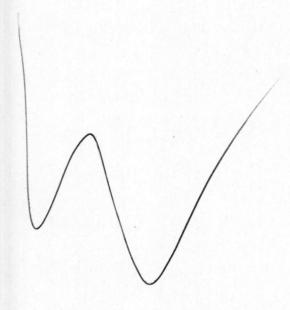

CODE OF THE KRILLITANES

Justin Richards

BBC LARGE PRINT

First published in 2010 by
BBC Books
This Large Print edition published 2010
by BBC Audiobooks by arrangement
with Ebury Press

ISBN 978 1 4056 2288 2

British Library Cataloguing in Publication Data available

Printed and bound in Great Britain by
CPI Antony Rowe, Chippenham and Eastbourne

CHAPTER ONE

It was a lovely sunny day, and something was very wrong indeed.

The Doctor thrust his hands deep into his jacket pockets and sniffed the London air. It smelled just as he expected, so there was nothing wrong there. Well, there was nothing more wrong than usual.

He set off down the street, nodding a greeting to a curious cat. He smiled at an old lady carrying shopping bags. She smiled back, then hurried on her way.

A few children were kicking a football about. The Doctor leaned against the end wall of a house and watched them for a while. The street ended in a small turning area where the ball bounced off the walls of houses. Two bundled sweatshirts marked out a goal.

The ball bounced off a wall and

rolled up to the Doctor. He picked it up and threw it back to a boy with spiky black hair, who ran after it. The boy was about 12 and had teeth that were still too big for his mouth.

'Training for the Olympics?' the Doctor asked.

'That's not for years yet,' the boy told him.

'Oh.' The Doctor was disappointed. 'I must be a bit early.' He licked his index finger and held it up to test the breeze. '2010, yes?'

The boy nodded. His friends had joined him and were watching the Doctor with interest.

'You're funny,' one of the other boys said.

'Very often,' the Doctor agreed.

The spiky-haired boy was eating crisps from a brightly coloured packet. He offered the Doctor one.

'No thanks. You have to be careful how much salt you eat, you know.'

The boy agreed. 'I know. Six grams is probably too much for an adult.

Nearly half the people in Britain go over that. The sodium is what does the damage. High blood pressure, risk of heart disease . . .'

The Doctor listened as the boy explained. He went into more and more detail about the dangers of eating too much salt. Then he paused to eat another crisp.

'Is he always like this?' the Doctor asked the other boys. 'He'll be explaining Einstein's Theory next.'

He had meant it as a joke, but the spiky-haired boy took this as an excuse to do exactly that. 'The "constant" that Einstein used was the speed of light,' the boy was saying as the Doctor stifled a yawn.

'Actually, I did know that,' he admitted.

The boy was talking faster and faster. Before long, he and the other boys had explained how to bypass Einstein. They knew how to design spaceships that could travel faster than light.

By this time, the Doctor had stopped yawning. 'Where do you go to school?' he asked.

Then he realised that the boys had gone back to their football. One of them loudly worked out the angle he would have to bounce the ball off one of the walls to get it in the goal. The Doctor frowned. The boy was exactly right.

A woman had come out of one of the houses and was watching the boys. The Doctor guessed that she was one of their mums.

'Clever kids,' he said, joining her.

The woman smiled. 'They're a good lot, really. At least they're playing footie, instead of bothering other people.'

'They bother me,' the Doctor said. 'Oh, not in a bad way. But the things they say are a bit worrying.'

The woman had a bag of crisps. It was the same brand as the boy had been eating. It had the same bright packaging. She offered the bag to the

Doctor, and this time he took one.

'They're good, aren't they? For crisps they're very, er, crisp.' The Doctor picked a bit of crisp from his teeth with his thumbnail. 'I was really looking for clues about the internet,' he went on.

'Oh?'

'My TARDIS links up to the local networks when it lands. It downloads news and weather and checks if I've won the lottery. That sort of thing.'

'That's useful.'

'Yes, very. Except, when I landed just now, it gave me a virus warning. For the whole internet. Everything. What's that all about?' He smiled and accepted another crisp. 'Sorry, ignore me.'

The woman smiled. 'So what's a TARDIS?'

'Time and Relative Dimension in Space. Don't worry about it.'

The Doctor watched the children kick their ball. One of them scored a goal, but another boy said he was offside.

'Which one's yours?' the Doctor asked.

The woman pointed to the spiky-haired boy. 'Spike,' she said.

'That makes sense. He was telling me how to build a spaceship. How did he know all that?'

The woman popped another crisp into her mouth. 'I blame these new Brainy Crisps. He's been too clever by half since he started eating them. I can't decide if I should be pleased or worried.'

'Brainy Crisps?' The Doctor could see now that the name was printed, big and bright, on the packet. 'Brainy Crisps.'

'They make you more brainy,' the woman explained. 'No one knows how they work, but if you ask me it must be based on a special protein molecule. It must attach itself to the red blood cells and carry extra oxygen to the brain . . .'

'Yes,' the Doctor said slowly. 'That

6

would work.'

'Not that I'd know,' the woman went on. 'I left school after my GCSEs, and I failed all of those. I can't even work the oven timer.' She crumpled the packet and stuffed it in her coat pocket.

The Doctor nodded, deep in thought. 'So, where do these Brainy Crisps come from?'

'We get ours from the supermarket.'

'That makes sense.' The Doctor smiled. 'It was nice talking to you. Thanks for the crisps.'

'No problem. I hope you get your TARDIS problem sorted.'

'So do I.'

'Of course,' the woman said, turning to go back indoors, 'the problem with Relative Dimensions is the Space-Time Gap. If you get that sorted, then you can time travel by simple Vortex-Jumping. Bye, then.'

The Doctor stared at the closed door for several minutes. When things got this weird, he decided, it was time to go shopping.

CHAPTER TWO

It was a while since the Doctor had been to a supermarket. He didn't generally need to go shopping. He had everything he needed in the TARDIS.

The supermarket was cool and bright with wide aisles. It wasn't too busy, and the Doctor wandered around, looking at the shelves. Supermarkets really did sell the strangest things, he thought.

There was even a whole display of televisions. They were hooked up to a camera that showed shoppers walking past. The Doctor paused to examine himself in widescreen. He drew back his lips to check his teeth. He stuck out his tongue, and was impressed with its colour and brightness. Moving on through the pizza aisle, he had to step aside to let a youth barge his trolley through.

Reaching the bread, the Doctor found his way blocked. A lady was unloading French sticks from a large wheeled bin.

'Can I help you, love?' she asked.

'Oh yes. I'm looking for crisps.' He leaned forward. 'Brainy Crisps,' he told her in a hushed whisper.

The woman took a step back. 'Looks like you need them.'

'I do,' the Doctor confessed. 'You have no idea.'

The woman nodded like she thought she had every idea. 'Three aisles down.'

'Thank you. You're very helpful,' the Doctor told her. 'They should give you a badge. "Helpful", it should say. A helpful badge for helpful people.'

The woman nodded. 'They're between the ketchup and the sweets.'

*　　*　　*

The Brainy Crisps were just where

the woman had said. The Doctor ignored the delights of lemon sherbets and wine gums. He glanced longingly at the jelly babies.

The crisp packets were the same as he had already seen. Their bright colours made them stand out on the shelf. There were multi-packs and individual bags. They were all on special offer, with two for the price of one, and extra Super Points.

'Bargain,' the Doctor murmured, picking up a bag.

He studied the ingredients list. It told him they were made of potato and vegetable oil and salt and flavouring. Which didn't really help.

'Made with actual ingredients,' it said below the list. That didn't help much, either.

The front of the packet said, 'Brainy Crisps—The snack that makes you Brainy!' On the back it told you how to go to the Brainy_Crisps website to test how much brainier you had got from eating the crisps. There was also, the Doctor noted, an address for comments or complaints.

So much for the sales pitch, he thought. Now to find out what was really going on. He stuck his sonic screwdriver between his teeth while he opened the bag of crisps.

The blue light from the sonic screwdriver lit up the inside of the packet. They certainly looked just like any other crisps. The Doctor checked the screwdriver's readings as he scanned the contents of the bag.

'Excuse me, Sunshine,' a gruff voice said.

The Doctor glanced up. He knew the voice wasn't talking to him. No one would call the Doctor 'Sunshine'.

A man in a blue suit was glaring at the Doctor from point-blank range. He was wearing a bright yellow badge. The badge said 'Derek', and under that it said 'Helpful'.

'I'm sorry, did you want to help

me?' the Doctor asked.

'What do you think you're doing, Sunshine?' Derek demanded.

The Doctor stared at him. '*I'm* Sunshine? You wear a badge that yellow and call *me* Sunshine?'

Derek sighed like he got this a lot. 'Have you paid for those crisps?' he asked.

'What crisps? Oh, these crisps? These crisps here?' The Doctor frowned. 'Er, not yet, actually. Not as such.'

'So that's a "no", then.'

'Yes. I mean, yes that's a no. I don't actually want to eat them,' the Doctor added. 'I'm just . . . looking.'

'You opened the packet,' Derek pointed out.

'Well, strictly speaking that is true.'

'So that's a "yes", then.'

The Doctor nodded. 'Excuse me, but is there a point to all this?'

'You want the crisps, you pay for them. Whether you want to eat them or just look at them, you pay for them, OK?'

'OK,' the Doctor decided. 'I'll take them.' He turned to survey the shelves of crisps. 'All of them.'

'Sorry?'

'All of them,' the Doctor said again. 'Every bag.'

'*Every* bag? Why?'

The Doctor grinned. 'They're on special offer. Now then, Helpful Derek, get us a trolley, would you?'

*   *   *

The Doctor needed two trolleys. He managed to get them to the checkout, pulling one and pushing the other. Each trolley was overflowing with Brainy Crisps.

'I wouldn't bother if it wasn't for the kids,' he told a man who was staring at him. The man's own trolley was full of cans of beer. 'What's your excuse?' the Doctor asked.

The Doctor chose the shortest queue. Even so, it seemed to take

14

longer than all the others. That didn't worry him. He knew there was a law that any queue you chose always moved slowest. It didn't matter how long it was. He even knew the formula for working out exactly how long it would take.

There was an old lady in front of the Doctor. Her hair was so white it looked slightly blue. Maybe that was the idea? She leaned heavily on her own trolley, which was almost empty. It held just four tins of cat food, some instant soup, and a small bar of chocolate.

'You sure you've got enough crisps?' the old lady asked the Doctor. Her eyes sparkled with amusement.

'I hope so,' the Doctor replied. 'Though to be honest, I'm not sure.'

'Those special offers are dangerous,' the old lady said. 'You always come away with something you didn't really want, and you always forget something that was on your list.'

The Doctor showed the old lady his psychic paper. It showed other people what the Doctor wanted them to see. 'I think I got everything on my list,' he said.

The old lady peered at the paper. 'It just says *crisps*.'

'Phew, that's all right then.' The Doctor made a point of looking into the old lady's trolley. 'You've not done so badly though. No impulse buys there.'

The old lady sniffed. 'Two for one, it's dangerous, I tell you. I mean, I don't even *have* a cat.'

They edged forward as a customer finished paying and left. The Doctor caught a rogue crisp bag as it fell. He stuffed it back into the trolley.

'If you ask me, they're a con,' the old lady said in a loud whisper.

'Two-for-one deals?'

'Those Brainy Crisps. A real con. I tried a bag yesterday,' she went on. 'No difference at all.'

'I'm sorry to hear that.'

'Now, if you've got a Super Card,' the old lady went on, 'that lot will earn you 548 points. Which is worth £2.74, the same as if they'd knocked 2p off every bag of crisps.'

'I wish I had a card, then.'

The old lady wasn't listening. 'It's all to do with getting cash moving. A discount doesn't keep the money in circulation, though it does get you to spend. A store card does both, so it's good for the economy. And of course every 2p you spend adds up to more. It goes into a bank which lends a part of it out to people who spend it again.'

Before the Doctor could interrupt, the old lady told him the formula for the speed of money moving round the economy. Then she explained the effects on the world stock markets—in detail, with numbers.

'And you don't even have a cat,' the Doctor murmured as the old lady

17

hunted through her purse for enough money to pay. She smiled a goodbye to the Doctor as she left.

'Do you have a Super Card?' the teenage girl on the checkout asked the Doctor when it was his turn.

'Sorry,' the Doctor said. 'Can you put it all on hers?' He pointed to the old lady as she trolleyed away.

The girl smiled, showing off metal braces on her teeth. 'I don't think the till will do that.'

The Doctor gave it a quick blast with his sonic screwdriver. 'It will now.'

'OK then.' She watched the Doctor unload his trolleys onto the checkout belt. 'You sure you need all those crisps?'

The Doctor could see the old lady leaving through the sliding doors at the other end of the shop. 'Oh yes,' he said. 'Quite sure.'

CHAPTER THREE

Two empty supermarket trolleys stood inside the TARDIS doors. Their contents—137 bags of crisps— were heaped up next to the main control console. The Doctor sat cross-legged on the floor beside the pile of crisp bags.

He took a bag from the pile. Other bags slid down the side, but he ignored them. He opened the bag of crisps and peered inside. He weighed it in his hand. He shone the light from his sonic screwdriver into the bag. He checked the chemical make-up of the crisps. He even ate one.

It was not an easy job working out what was special about the crisps. There were lots of tests the Doctor had to do. Some he could use the sonic screwdriver for, others he could not. Before long, the TARDIS floor was strewn with bits of equipment. There were read-outs and dials and handsets and detectors. There were lots and lots of empty crisp packets.

After about an hour, the Doctor had the information he needed. It had taken fifty-four bags of crisps, which meant he had a large pile left over. He would worry about what to do with them later. For now he had something else to worry about.

He had discovered two things. The first, to be honest, he could have found out without opening a single bag. It was the name and address of the firm that made the crisps. The address was printed on the back of every packet.

The other thing he had discovered was what the crisps were fried in. It was Krillitane Oil. He tapped the end of the sonic screwdriver gently against his teeth as he thought about this. The more he thought about it, the more it worried him.

Last time he had met the

Krillitanes in this time period, they were frying school chips in their oil. It certainly made the human brain work harder and faster, but it was hardly safe. The oil itself was highly inflammable and could even explode. The Krillitanes themselves were allergic to their own oil. If it touched their leathery skin, they burned or blew up.

As an alien race, the Krillitanes were interesting. They were not very nice, but they were interesting. They could make themselves look like ordinary people. Their true form changed over the years as they absorbed the qualities and traits of the races they conquered. At the moment, at this stage of their evolution, they were like giant walking bats, with wings and claws and very sharp teeth.

The Doctor sucked air through his own teeth. What were the Krillitanes up to this time? Before, they had taken over just one school and fed the children brainy chips. Back then they were trying to find the formula that controlled the universe.

How much more dangerous could things be now if they were feeding Krillitane Oil to everyone in the country? Did it even stop at Britain—what if the firm was exporting its crisps all over the world? The scale of the plan meant it was hugely dangerous.

There were lots of questions, the Doctor thought to himself. But at least the crisp bags had told him where to start looking for the answers.

*   *   *

The crisp firm occupied a large office block on the outskirts of London. Miss Sark always told Maddie on the front desk if a new person was expected to arrive to start work. So Maddie was a bit surprised by the words of the tall, thin man with unruly dark hair. He grinned at her and said he was here to start work.

'There's nothing in my online diary about you starting—Mr . . .?' She prompted him for his name.

'Smith. And it's Doctor, in fact. Doctor John Smith.'

The man leaned across the front desk and turned the display screen so he could see it. He was holding what might have been a pen, though the end glowed bright blue.

'Ah, here it is. That's me.'

Maddie couldn't understand how she'd missed it. There on the screen of today's expected visitors was 'Doctor John Smith—Strategy and Workflow Manager (Access All Areas)'.

'I'd better sort you out a badge, sir.'

'Just Doctor will do,' he told her. 'You've been a great help. I'll be sure to tell whoever you work for.'

'Miss Sark,' Maddie told him,

handing him a clip-on ID badge. 'This will do till we get you a proper one with your picture on it. Miss Sark is Sir Manning Cross's own assistant, but I expect you know that.'

The Doctor pinned on his temporary Access All Areas badge. 'I expect I do,' he agreed.

*   *   *

It took the Doctor a little while to arrange himself an office. He made sure it had a computer, phone, pot plants, and a framed painting of a steam train in the rain, by JMW Turner. He also had an in-tray with nothing in it, and an out-tray with nothing in that either.

A few people asked the Doctor who he was and what he did. When he told them he was the new manager for Strategy and Workflow, their eyes glazed over slightly and they changed the subject. They were all used to managers who did nothing anyone understood—or perhaps who just did nothing.

The next stage was to get himself along to a few meetings. Then he could find out what the people who did do things actually did. There was an online diary which told the Doctor there was a Management Team Briefing in half an hour in Meeting Room 6D. That sounded useful.

A young woman with long fair hair and rectangular glasses was working at a desk close to the door of the Doctor's office.

'Excuse me,' he asked, 'but where's Meeting Room 6D?'

She paused from her rattle of frantic typing to give him directions.

'Thank you, er . . .?' He tried to read her name from her badge, but the print was too small.

'I'm Gabby.'

'Of course. Nice to meet you, Gabby.' The Doctor turned to go.

'I'm your secretary,' Gabby added, to the Doctor's surprise.

'I have a secretary?'

'All high-level managers have a secretary.'

'Well, I hope you have enough to keep you occupied for now.'

Gabby smiled nervously, as if she was not sure if he was joking. 'There's loads. You've got over fifty emails to deal with, and there are reports to sign off. Plus expenses claims, and the group budget needs final numbers by Thursday.'

The Doctor nodded. 'I didn't know I was so busy. Keep up the good work. If anyone wants me, I'll be . . .' He pointed vaguely in the direction Gabby had told him. 'This way for 6D, right?'

*   *   *

He took the lift up to the sixth floor. There were several other people heading towards Meeting Room 6D.

The men were dressed smartly in suits, with flashy ties and well-polished shoes. The women were in dark, stylish business clothes and designer shoes.

The Doctor paused in the doorway. He looked round the large glass table as everyone else took their seats. Then he glanced down at his crumpled suit and trainers. They were still muddy from the jungles of the planet Coco-Notix Five.

'You must be the Doctor,' a stern female voice said from behind him. 'Go on in—we've been expecting you.'

CHAPTER FOUR

The woman who ushered the Doctor into the meeting room was as tall as he was but much broader. Her dark hair was cut above the collar like she was a schoolboy. Her dark jacket strained to do up.

'Stella Sark,' she introduced herself. 'You know, I'm surprised I didn't interview you for this job. Usually Sir Manning asks me to meet all the management recruits.'

'Perhaps it was your day off,' the Doctor said. 'So, you're the famous Stella Sark? May I call you—'

'Miss Sark,' she told him. 'Yes, you may.'

'Miss Sark,' the Doctor echoed. 'It has a ring to it.'

He found himself a chair between two men in smart suits.

'This is cosy,' he said to them. 'Do we get biscuits? Custard creams are

28

the best. Or those ones that look like they've got squashed flies stuck in them.'

Neither of the men said anything, so the Doctor held out his hand to one of them. 'Garibaldi,' he remembered the squashed fly biscuits were called.

The man shook his hand. 'Edward Howell. Pleased to meet you, Gary.'

It took the Doctor a moment to work it out. Then he laughed. 'Oh, sorry. No—I'm not Gary. Imagine being called Gary Baldie, especially if you had no hair. That'd be something, wouldn't it? No, no, no, just call me Doctor.'

He turned to the man on the other side of him. 'Sorry, didn't catch your name.'

'Gary,' the man said. He was completely bald.

The Doctor's eyes widened.

'Joke,' the man explained, breaking into a grin. 'It's Clive.'

Someone cleared their throat very

loudly. It was Stella Sark, now standing at the end of the large table. The Doctor realised that she and everyone else was looking at him and the man who wasn't called Gary.

'If you are all quite ready?' Miss Sark said. 'We have a lot to get through today. Sir Manning will join us for the closing summary in an hour.'

The Doctor shielded his mouth from Miss Sark and asked Clive in a loud whisper: 'Sir Manning Cross, is that?'

Clive nodded, while trying to look as though he had not heard the Doctor. Though everyone else at the table had.

'He's my boss,' the Doctor whispered proudly.

'No, Doctor,' Miss Sark said. 'Sir Manning is *my* boss. And I am yours.'

The Doctor nodded and raised his hand to show he'd understood. 'Of course, but he's sort of my boss too, isn't he? Well,' he went on, 'I guess he's all our bosses really. Can we do that thing where we go round the table?'

Miss Sark blinked, thrown by the change of subject.

'I don't mean musical chairs,' the Doctor said quickly.

'Well, that's a mercy,' Miss Sark said.

'Though musical chairs might be fun. No, I mean, you know, go round the table and introduce ourselves. I'll start. I'm the Doctor. I'm a bit new, well I only started today actually. I'm managing Workflow and Strategy, er, stuff. Anyway, I'm settling in nicely, thank you. Everyone's being very helpful.' He nudged Clive. 'Right, your turn.'

'I think the rest of us know each other,' Miss Sark said coldly. 'Perhaps we can introduce ourselves over coffee. At the coffee break,' she added, in case the Doctor saw this as an excuse to get coffee now.

'Just so long as I don't feel left out,' the Doctor agreed. 'That all right with you, Clive?'

* * *

The hour until the coffee break was one of the most boring the Doctor could recall, but he didn't complain. He tried not to yawn too often.

When Miss Sark went through the monthly budget figures, he began to get interested. The spending on the Computer Department was far higher than he had expected.

When Miss Sark showed the numbers of hits on the Brainy_Crisps website, the Doctor was more than surprised—he was astonished. He whistled through his teeth.

'Impressed, Doctor?' Miss Sark asked.

'Gobsmacked, Miss Sark.'

'You shouldn't be. The website is a key part of our strategy. As the manager handling Strategy and

Workflow, I'd expect you to know that.'

'I'm gobsmacked that we get all those people visiting the website, and haven't found a way of making money from it. What sort of strategy is that?' The Doctor leaned forward. 'Or is it that maybe—just maybe—making money isn't what we are trying to do?'

Miss Sark's eyes narrowed. 'Moving swiftly on to more pressing matters,' she said, 'I'd like to talk about the window-cleaning contract . . .'

*   *   *

Sir Manning Cross was a contrast to Miss Sark. He slipped into the room almost unnoticed. He was a tall, lean man with a hooked nose and deep-set eyes. The Doctor saw him standing at the side of the room, watching as Miss Sark ended her talk. Sir Manning caught the

Doctor's eye, and for the briefest moment he looked puzzled. Then he smiled. The Doctor smiled back.

Miss Sark sat down, and Sir Manning walked to the head of the table. 'Thank you, Miss Sark. An excellent job, as ever. I just wanted to say, very quickly, that this month's figures are even better than last month's. My thanks to all of you for that. Our plan is on track, on time, and on budget.'

'Plan?' the Doctor asked.

'Business plan,' Miss Sark told him sharply.

Sir Manning did not seem to hear either of them. 'Now, if there are no questions . . .' It was clear he didn't expect any. He frowned. 'Yes?'

The Doctor had his hand up. 'Sorry, is it only me? Just one very quick question, if I may? That wasn't the question, by the way.'

'Yes?' Sir Manning prompted.

'Why are we spending so much on the computers? Well, there's the website, I know about that. There's the special factory producing the Brainy Crisps. There's the firm's systems and all that. Still, I think it's an awful lot of money.'

Sir Manning tilted his head to one side as he considered. It made him look like a hawk eyeing up its prey. 'It's good to invest in new technology,' he said at last. 'It's good to look to the future, don't you think?'

'Always,' the Doctor agreed. 'That doesn't really answer my question, though, does it?'

'You have so many questions.' Sir Manning clicked his tongue thoughtfully. 'But that isn't a bad thing. The person you need to talk to is Henry. He's in charge of the computer systems.'

'Henry?' The Doctor looked round the table. But no one owned up to being Henry.

'He doesn't come to these meetings,' Miss Sark said. 'I have no

35

idea why.'

'Perhaps he finds them a bit boring and useless,' the Doctor said lightly. 'Just a thought.'

*   *   *

Ten minutes later, the meeting room was empty apart from Sir Manning and Miss Sark.

'So who is he?' Sir Manning wanted to know.

'The Doctor—Doctor Smith. He is the new Manager for Strategy and Workflow.'

Sir Manning raised an eyebrow. 'I didn't know we had a new Manager for Strategy and Workflow.'

'Neither did I. I thought you must have hired him.'

Sir Manning shook his head. 'I don't even know what Strategy and Workflow means—and neither does he, I suspect.'

'It could be some sort of mix-up,' Miss Sark said. 'He seems harmless enough.'

Sir Manning's mouth twitched in what might have been a smile. 'And you seem human enough. Looks can deceive. We know that more than anyone.'

'Do you want him dealt with?'

'If he's here to make trouble, it's clear what his next move will be.'

Miss Sark smiled. 'Of course. He'll go and see Henry.'

Sir Manning Cross was smiling too. 'I think we can let Henry deal with him.'

CHAPTER FIVE

Gabby was happy to set up a meeting with Henry, who was Director of Computing. He turned out to be a middle-aged man with thinning dark hair and a beer belly. He was wearing a suit. The Doctor could tell from the stains what Henry had eaten every day for the last week.

Henry brought his 'Number Two' with him. This was a spotty youth called Jeff. He had long greasy hair and was wearing jeans. He looked more like someone on work experience than the deputy to a director. Both of them seemed nervous and awkward as the Doctor waved them to chairs in his office.

'So what's the problem?' Henry asked.

'I didn't say there was a problem,' the Doctor pointed out.

Jeff laughed. 'No one wants to see

us unless there's a problem. What is it? Can't you log in? Is your screen frozen? Are you getting an error message that makes no sense?'

The Doctor shook his head. 'None of the above. I'm fine. I just wanted to have a chat, really. See how it's going. Find out what I can do to help.'

'Find out what you can do—to help *us*?' Henry said. The way he looked at Jeff and the way Jeff looked at him suggested that this was new thinking.

'Well, there was one other thing,' the Doctor admitted.

'Ah,' Henry said.

'Knew it,' Jeff muttered.

'I'd like you to tell me all about the computer systems you have here. You have a huge budget, so what do you spend it on? How much digital power do you have here, and how is it used?'

Both Henry and Jeff were staring at the Doctor open-mouthed. Their surprise turned to complete astonishment when the Doctor added, 'I'm interested.'

* * *

Before long, Henry and Jeff were chatting with the Doctor like old friends. He soon had a good idea of how the computer systems worked. He was right—the food firm had a much bigger computer system than it would need just to make crisps. Whatever the Krillitanes were up to, the computer systems must be vital to it.

The Doctor also realised that Henry and Jeff were both good at their jobs. At least, Henry was great at the technical aspects. He didn't sound like he could really cope with the management role he'd been given. It was a classic case of someone promoted to the point where they were out of their depth.

Jeff took over the Doctor's

computer and began to show him some of the firm's systems. He displayed plans of the computer network, and lists of computer servers. He showed the amount of work each one did and how the jobs were shared out and balanced across the network.

'So most of the computing power is linked in to the Brainy_Crisps website,' the Doctor said.

'That's right,' Jeff agreed.

'But surely it doesn't need that much power. Not even with all the people who visit the site.'

'The computers have to handle the tests the people do,' Henry said. 'But you're right. It's strange, we keep adding more and more computer power and still it doesn't seem to be enough to process all the data that comes back.'

'It's almost as if that data was a lot more than just simple test results,' the Doctor said. 'I think there's more to this website than the three of us understand.'

Jeff laughed. 'It's just a website with some simple tests so people can check if they've got any more brainy after eating the crisps.'

Henry, however, was nodding. 'That's what I think, Doctor. I'm not stupid,' he went on, 'and neither is Sir Manning Cross, but he's given me a job that I'm not really any good at. I have to wonder if that's on purpose, and if so—why?'

'To stop you looking too closely at what's going on, perhaps,' the Doctor said. 'And to act as a front man, to head off nosy people like me. Unless, of course, you already know what's going on and this is all a bluff.'

Jeff was shaking his head. 'We all know what's going on. It's a website, that's all. So it takes a bit more power to run it than we thought. That's no surprise really. It's not the end of the world.'

The Doctor looked him in the eye.

'I hope you're right about that.'

There was a moment of silence. Then the Doctor clapped his hands together, coming to a decision.

'This website is the key to everything. So let's have a look at it. Fire it up, please, Jeff. I'm going to take the Brainy Test.'

*　　　*　　　*

'OK, so it's a bit weird,' Jeff had to admit later.

It was dark outside, and everyone else seemed to have gone home.

The Doctor had taken the test. At first it was all simple and what he had been expecting—a few sums, some missing words to fill in, some spot-the-next-shape-in-the-sequence puzzles, and so on.

After a while, though, the tests changed. It was as if the website had got to know the Doctor was clever enough to solve harder problems.

It was not a sudden change. The

Doctor gradually found that he was getting more and more questions he wouldn't expect in a normal test. There were really quite tricky questions about DNA and the way it was made. There were boxes where he had to fill in sums to work out how evolution took place. There were problems to solve that the Doctor knew no human being could have devised—or understood.

But the people who had eaten the Brainy Crisps would be able to do them. This was not a test. This was real, new research on a massive scale.

'How many people use this website?' the Doctor asked.

'At any time there are over half a million users on the network,' Jeff said.

'That's a lot of computer power.'

'You know how much,' Henry said. 'We told you earlier.'

'I didn't mean the machines, I meant the people doing the test.'

The Doctor sat back and thought about his next move. 'So, who devised this test? Who set it up?'

'The web pages were already built,' Jeff said. 'We were given the questions, and we just had to put them on the server so people could get to them on the internet.'

The Doctor clicked on the web browser. He got back into the firm's systems and found a way into the secure Accounts area.

'How did you do that?' Jeff asked, impressed.

'It's a knack,' the Doctor said modestly. 'I was thinking there must be a payment record. Whoever built the website got paid, or had their time billed to it, so there must be a note of that.'

He found the right folder for the website work, but it refused to open.

'Problem?' Henry asked.

'Looks like higher management has its own network within the main firm's systems.'

'That's right. Even we aren't allowed access to that.'

'Can you get into it, Doctor?' Jeff asked eagerly.

The Doctor shook his head. 'It's protected by a digital deadlock seal. There's no way in, even for me. Well, not unless I destroy the whole system, and that seems a bit extreme. Who would have access?'

'To the whole system?' Henry said. 'Only Sir Manning Cross.'

The Doctor leaped to his feet. 'Then we need to use his computer. I'll be able to bypass the seal from there. Then we can get into his personal network and data.'

'Isn't that a bit naughty?' Henry asked.

'Oh yes. Let's do it. He'll be long gone by now. I hope.' The Doctor turned to Jeff. 'Can I ask you to stay here and keep an eye on the systems? I need to know if anyone else detects us getting inside the network. Keep an eye out for any unusual activity—can you do that?'

'Sure thing, Doctor.'

*   *   *

It was the end of the day, and the offices were dark and empty. Henry led the Doctor to Sir Manning Cross's office on the seventh floor. It took only a moment for the Doctor to open the door, and they slipped inside.

'Are you all right if I go and set some things going in my office?' Henry asked. 'We run some of the accounts programs at night. That way we don't disrupt the systems while people are working.'

The Doctor was happy to be left to hack into Sir Manning's computer. He sat alone in the near-darkness, his face lit by the glow from the screen. The rest of the office was a jungle of shadows. Soon the Doctor was lost in his work, breaking the digital deadlock seal and hacking into the management systems.

'Now we're getting somewhere,' he murmured. He glanced up, embarrassed at having said it out loud, but there was nobody in the room to hear him.

*   *   *

The office the Doctor had been given was filled with shadows. Jeff's face was lit up by the glow from the screen as he worked.

A draught shifted the papers on the desk. A deeper, darker shadow fell across him, and Jeff looked up.

'Oh,' he said, relieved, 'it's just you. I thought you'd gone. Did you forget something?'

The shadow changed shape as the creature that cast it started to transform into its true body. Jeff stood up, mouth open in fear. He beat at the figure looming over him, trying to fend it off. The chair toppled over behind him. Jeff caught hold of something and pulled. It came away, but he had no time to wonder what was in his hand.

Huge, leathery wings beat the air, scattering papers. A high-pitched shriek drowned out Jeff's cry of terror. Sharp, alien claws slashed down.

Jeff's lifeless body slumped to the floor. The beating of wings stopped and the shadow shrank back to its original size. A hand that once again looked human closed the door.

CHAPTER SIX

The Doctor was getting bored. He had been through so many files that the screen was starting to blur before his eyes. Despite his hopes, he had actually found very little of interest.

'Any luck?' Henry asked, stepping back into the room.

The Doctor leaned back and stretched. He peered at Henry's dim shape in the gloom. 'Not much, I'm afraid. Most of it is the sort of rubbish management reports we got at the meeting today.'

'That's why I stopped going. That and the way they always seemed to find fault with what I was doing. They said it was too slow, or too costly, or just plain wrong. I know I'm not really very good at my job, but they put me in it. They could at least help.'

'There was one thing,' the Doctor

confessed. He shut down the computer and turned off the screen. 'There's a company meeting tomorrow morning.'

'We have so many meetings in this place. It's amazing anyone has time between them to get any real work done.'

The Doctor grinned in the near-darkness. 'But this meeting is at seven in the morning. It's in a posh hotel, and it's not in Sir Manning's diary. There's no agenda, and no list of who is attending. There's just a time and an address in a coded email from Miss Sark.'

'A secret meeting,' Henry said. 'I wonder what it's about.'

'The coded email says it's been called by the firm's main shareholders. I'm hoping it's about what's really going on.'

'Doctor—what *is* really going on?' Henry sounded annoyed. 'I don't know who you are or what you're doing here. You tell me the computers are running some secret program that's linked to the Brainy_Crisps website. So what? Why are we sneaking about in the dark, breaking into the boss's office and hacking his computer?'

The Doctor walked slowly round the office. He peered into corners and opened drawers and cupboards. 'What if I told you the Brainy Crisps are bad for you? What if I told you that eating them makes you clever but slowly burns away your brain? Would you believe me?'

'I might,' Henry said. 'I have wondered what side effects there might be. I mean, if the science exists to make everyone brainy, why can't you get it on the NHS? It can't cost too much because it's as cheap as crisps.'

The Doctor found a pile of papers in a drawer and started leafing through them. 'What if I told you that the science—the brainy formula, if you like—is secret. It's known only

52

to Sir Manning Cross and Miss Sark and a few others?' He closed the drawer and moved to a door at the side of the room.

The door was locked. It couldn't lead anywhere as it was close to the building's outside wall, and the Doctor guessed it opened into a storeroom. Maybe useful files were locked away inside.

'Well, I suppose that makes sense,' Henry said. 'But why waste it just making crisps?'

The Doctor set to work on the door with his sonic screwdriver. 'What if I told you that Sir Manning and Miss Sark know the secret because they're not human?'

'Not human?' Henry joined the Doctor by the door. 'What do you mean, not human?'

'Aliens,' the Doctor whispered. He slipped the sonic screwdriver back into his jacket pocket.

'Aliens? Selling crisps?!'

'A means to an end. They disguise

themselves as humans.'

Henry took a deep breath. 'So what do they really look like, these aliens?'

The Doctor pulled the door open. There was just enough light to see what was inside. 'Um,' the Doctor said quietly. 'Well . . . They look exactly like that, in fact.'

Inside the small room behind the door, hung the dark shape of a Krillitane. The huge, winged creature was hanging upside down from the ceiling. Its wings were folded round its body. The long head looked like it was carved from brittle stone.

'Is it asleep?' Henry asked in a hushed whisper.

The creature opened its eyes. 'No,' it said.

The Doctor slammed the door shut. He whipped out his sonic screwdriver and aimed it at the lock. 'Time we were going.'

Henry didn't move. He was

standing frozen with fear.

The Doctor pushed him roughly towards the office door. 'Run!'

Behind them, the door to the storeroom exploded into splinters. The Krillitane smashed its way out, and set off after the Doctor and Henry. It took long lolloping strides. Once in the open-plan area outside Sir Manning's office, it opened its wings.

Henry and the Doctor ran for their lives. They could hear Krillitane wings beating behind them. The creature was half running, half flying. It bounded after them, launching itself forward from panels and walls. Its screeches filled the air.

'Where are we going?' Henry gasped. He was having trouble keeping up with the Doctor. He was also having trouble seeing where they were going.

'Who knows?' the Doctor shouted back. Then: 'Ah!' He suddenly dived sideways down an aisle between desks.

Henry almost fell as he turned to follow. The Krillitane was close on his heels. Ahead of him, the Doctor had grabbed something from a wall mount—a fire extinguisher.

The Doctor brought the fire extinguisher up, aiming the hose at the Krillitane. Henry dived to one side as the Doctor pressed the lever. The Krillitane shrieked louder as it saw what was happening. It launched itself through the air at the Doctor. A jet of carbon dioxide gas gushed out over the Krillitane. It caught the creature full in the face, the pressure knocking it backwards.

The Doctor stepped forward, still spraying. As soon as the fire extinguisher ran out, he dropped it. He shouted again at Henry to run.

The Krillitane was thrashing in pain. It struggled to get up.

The Doctor and Henry now had enough time to get away. The Doctor let Henry lead the way since he knew his way round the offices.

'Fire stairs,' Henry suggested. 'We need to warn Jeff about these alien creatures.'

Soon they were back at the Doctor's office.

'How many of those things are there?' Henry asked as they went inside.

'More than one, clearly,' the Doctor said sadly.

Jeff's body lay stretched out across the floor. The Doctor checked it briefly, but he could tell at once that the man was dead.

'Poor Jeff,' he said quietly. 'I am so sorry.'

Henry was standing in the doorway, his face pale in the light cast by the computer screen.

The Doctor stood up and walked slowly over to Henry. 'When you left me in Sir Manning's office,' he said coldly, 'it was only for a few minutes. But you had time to come back here.'

Henry nodded. 'If only I had. I might have been here when . . .' He looked away. 'I might have been able to save him.' A single tear escaped from one of Henry's eyes and rolled down his cheek. 'Is that what you mean?'

The Doctor watched the tear glisten on Henry's cheek. Did Krillitanes cry, he wondered. 'That's what I mean, yes,' he said. 'And you couldn't have saved him, not from a Krillitane. You mustn't blame yourself for this.'

Henry turned back to the Doctor. His face was determined. He brushed away the tear with the back of his hand. 'What do we do, Doctor? How do we stop these monsters before they kill anyone else?'

'First we need to know what they're up to. I hope we'll find that out at the secret meeting at the hotel tomorrow.' The Doctor leaned forwards suddenly, staring at Henry.

'You haven't had your ears pierced, have you?'

'No, why?'

The Doctor ran his hand through his hair, spiking it up. 'Just wondered.'

'Right,' Henry said, confused. 'But even if we know their plan, what can we do against something that can . . . ?' Henry's voice tailed off and he glanced again at Jeff's body.

'Well,' the Doctor said, leading Henry out of his office, 'it's not all gloom and doom, you know. I mean, I still have eighty-three bags of crisps.'

CHAPTER SEVEN

The Doctor and Henry wanted to be at the hotel ahead of everyone else. They arrived at six and found that the staff were already setting things up for the meeting. The Doctor showed them his psychic paper, which appeared to say that he and Henry were meant to be there to check that everything was running smoothly and on time.

The meeting was going to take place in the ballroom. The middle of the room had been cleared and a single long table set up. High above it was a net, full of brightly coloured balloons. Everything was ready and waiting for a silver wedding party in the evening. Tables and chairs were stacked on one side of the room, also ready for later.

'I love parties,' the Doctor told Henry, as they looked up at the net.

'Don't you?'

'I don't get invited to many,' Henry admitted. 'What are you thinking?'

The Doctor told him. Henry assumed he was joking, but the Doctor wasn't.

Half an hour later, the Doctor pulled Henry quickly to one side. A young woman with blonde hair and glasses had just come into the ballroom. The Doctor and Henry crouched down out of sight. They hid themselves behind the stack of tables and chairs at the side of the room.

'It's only Gabby,' Henry said. 'They often get her to hand out the coffee and information packs at meetings. She's good with people.'

'I'd rather no one knew we were here, even Gabby,' the Doctor told him. 'Besides, she might tell me off for not getting into work early to catch up on my emails.'

'So what do we do now—just wait here?'

'For the moment.' The Doctor was

holding a small remote control box he had found. It controlled the lights and curtains and a few other things in the room. He was hoping Sir Manning Cross wouldn't notice it was gone. 'We need to find a good place to hide, and we have a little job to do.'

Soon, the first people started arriving for the meeting. Gabby handed out folders and showed people where they could help themselves to coffee and tea. There were glasses and bottles of water on the table.

By seven o'clock, everyone had taken their seats. Sir Manning Cross and Stella Sark sat at one end of the big table. The Doctor could see Clive and a few other people from yesterday's meeting. Gabby spoke quietly to Stella Sark, then left the room. She closed the door firmly behind her.

There were half a dozen other people, too. They were not dressed as uniformly as the men and women from the firm. One of them was a large man with steel-grey hair and a military moustache. He took charge and opened the meeting. The man introduced himself as James Purcell, although everyone seemed to know him already.

'You may be wondering why I asked for this meeting of the firm's board and our most important shareholders,' Purcell said. 'Well, it's quite simple really. Since Sir Manning took charge, we've seen the firm's profits rocket. These new Brainy Crisps really seem to be doing very well.'

Sir Manning smiled. 'So you've called us here to give us your thanks, I take it.'

'Well, yes. And no.'

'Oh? I thought the point of any firm was to make profit.'

Purcell scowled. 'The point of any firm is to make profit for its shareholders. But despite the huge amounts of money the firm is making, you are still not paying out to shareholders.'

Stella Sark leaned forward. 'The value of your shares has gone up a lot. Isn't that enough?'

'Frankly, no. I don't want to sell my shares. Why would I, when everything is going so well. What I want is to see some return on my investment. Instead, you seem hell-bent on putting all the profits back into ever more costly IT projects. Computer projects which we just don't need.'

There were murmurs of agreement from the other share-holders. Someone clapped.

Sir Manning rose to his feet. 'I rather think it is up to me to decide what is necessary. I run this firm.'

Purcell gave a snort of laughter. 'We *own* this firm. You work for us.'

'Not any more,' Miss Sark said, so quietly that Purcell didn't seem to hear.

'You have no idea, do you,' Sir Manning said. His voice was rising in pitch and volume. 'No idea at all what we are really doing. How dare you presume to tell me how to run my firm?'

'*Our* firm,' Purcell said, but he was hesitant now. He seemed surprised at Sir Manning's sudden anger.

'You thought you could make a quick few pounds out of potato crisps and gullible customers,' Sir Manning ranted. 'That's all you were in it for. Well, no longer. Your involvement ends, here and now.'

The shareholders looked at each other, surprised and confused.

'Is he offering to buy us out?' a woman in a blue dress asked the man beside her.

'All you think about is money,' Sir Manning told her. 'I am trying to create *life*!'

There was silence. Everyone stared at Sir Manning.

'Now we're getting somewhere,'

the Doctor whispered to Henry as they watched from their hiding place.

'You heard me—*life*!' Sir Manning looked round the table. 'That's why we needed your money, and why we now need every penny of profit. We have done what no other firm can do. We have hijacked the internet.'

Purcell stared in utter surprise. 'What?!'

'That's right. When any computer links to the Brainy_Crisps website, it is instantly infected with our code. The code links infected computers together over the internet, then finds and links in every other computer, too. Oh, we only steal a little bit of computing power from each one, but hundreds of millions of computers are working away for us. They are working on the equations and formulae provided by the people who have eaten our crisps.'

Miss Sark stood beside her boss. 'Almost everyone who eats Brainy Crisps goes to our website to find out how much more brainy they've become. They think they're playing a game, or answering a pop-up question. They think they're rating the usefulness of the site and the tastiness of the crisps. In fact, they are all slowly solving the overall problem. They are solving it with improved intelligence from the Brainy Crisps and the processing power of the entire internet.'

Purcell and the other shareholders were really confused now. 'But why? What problem are they solving?'

Sir Manning smiled. 'The computers work *with* the people whose brains have been improved by the oil in the crisps. Together they are solving the riddle of life itself. We are a race that has evolved in a random way. We have chosen a hotchpotch of bits and pieces from other life forms. Over the years, this has become inefficient. We have lost our way. Even the oil we secrete is a poison to us. It burns us when we touch it—our own oil. Now we will redesign ourselves to be the greatest, most powerful species in the universe.'

'I think we've heard quite enough,' Purcell said. 'I had no idea when we gave you the job that you were a complete madman. It's time to propose a motion that we remove you from the firm at once.'

Behind the stack of tables and chairs, the Doctor turned to Henry. His face looked grave. 'So that's what they're doing. The Krillitanes are creating a new genetic form for themselves. Up to now they've been evolving over time. They've taken parts that seemed useful and random bits of DNA from the species they've conquered. Now they've decided to design themselves again, and to do it properly from scratch.'

'Is that bad?' Henry asked.

'Not if they were a nice, friendly race of cuddly creatures. But they're not. They're warlike empire-builders who'll enslave the human race and any other species as soon as look at them.'

The shareholders were nodding, about to vote on Purcell's motion. Then Miss Sark walked round the table and grabbed Purcell. The other shareholders watched in horror as Stella Sark lifted Purcell off the floor. She flung him across the table, and glasses and bottles and papers went flying.

'Time, I think, for our investors to see what they have really bought,' Sir Manning said.

The people from the firm all stood up. There were about eight of them, including Sir Manning, Stella, and Clive. The air around them shimmered and blurred. Then, in place of the people, stood tall winged creatures with long stony faces and sharp claws. Krillitanes.

'Now,' the Krillitane that had been Sir Manning Cross snarled, 'are there any questions before you die?'

The shareholders sat frozen in terror. Purcell was groaning as he pulled himself off the table. Only one person spoke.

'Um, since you ask, yes. I have a question.'

Henry looked on in horror as the Doctor stood up and walked towards the table.

'Yes, me again, I'm afraid, and I have another question. I just can't help myself. It's how I am. So, I was just wondering . . .'

The Krillitanes all watched the Doctor.

'I assume you're planning to create a race of Super-Krillitane creatures ready to make Earth their first new home world. And from there take over—well, maybe one day—the whole universe. Is that right?'

The air was filled with alien laughter.

'I shall answer your question, Doctor—your *last* question,' the Krillitane Stella Sark said. 'The

70

answer is yes.'

'Let me ask *you* a question,' Sir Manning said.

The Doctor nodded happily. 'Oh good, I like a good question. Which came first, the chicken or the egg? The egg, definitely. Or was it the chicken? Sorry, what's the question?'

'Simply this. We are going to kill all the people in this room, Doctor, starting with you. Then we are going to complete our plan and conquer this world. So, I ask you this: what can you possibly hope to do about it?'

The Doctor stuck his hands into his pockets. He sucked air through his teeth. Finally, he grinned. 'Well,' he said, 'I can offer you a crisp.'

CHAPTER EIGHT

The Doctor faced the Krillitanes.

The human shareholders were trapped in their seats. They were too afraid to move. But even if they did, the Krillitanes had them trapped. The people would be cut down before they got to the door to escape.

'You are a very strange human being, Doctor,' said the Krillitane Sir Manning.

'Oh, I'm not a human being at all,' the Doctor told him. 'Which means you have a choice to make, because I'm giving you a last chance.'

The Krillitane's large head dipped slightly as it laughed. '*You* are giving *us* a last chance?'

'Better believe it.' The Doctor was serious. Slowly the alien laughter died away. When there was silence, the Doctor said, 'One last chance.

Leave now. Give up on this daft plan of yours. Be happy with what you've got and accept how you are.'

'Strange and stupid, it would seem,' Stella Sark said. 'Do you really expect us to listen to you, whoever you really are?'

The Doctor shook his head sadly. 'No, not really.'

'Then I am afraid the party is over,' Sir Manning said.

'Oh no,' the Doctor told him. 'It's only just starting. I warned you,' he said, pointing to the Krillitanes. Then he pointed to the human shareholders cowering in their seats. 'And you lot—run!'

In his free hand, the Doctor was holding the remote control he had found earlier. He pressed one of the buttons. High above the large glass table, the net full of balloons dropped away. The balloons fell like a multicoloured blanket.

Something else was falling, too— the contents of eighty-three bags of

Brainy Crisps. The Doctor and Henry had opened the bags and attached them inside the net before the meeting started. As the net opened, the bags tipped and the crisps fell. They rained down past the slowly falling balloons. Crisps scattered across the table, the floor, the humans and the Krillitanes.

A crisp landed on the leathery arm of one of the Krillitanes. The crisp exploded as the oil in it reacted with the alien's skin. Crisps burst into flames, filling the room with flashes of light. The Krillitanes shrieked in pain, reeling away from the table as the crisps rained down.

Stella Sark rolled on the floor, frantic to put out the fire burning along her back. Sir Manning Cross's body was a patchwork of black and orange. Crisps exploded and burned. The room was filled with smoke.

While they set the trap with the crisps, the Doctor had told Henry it was his job to help everyone out of the room. As soon as the Doctor pressed the button, Henry ran to open the doors and herd everyone out. The Doctor pushed Purcell and the other shareholders ahead of him. Together with Henry, he bundled them out of the room. Once outside, Henry slammed the doors shut behind them and the Doctor locked them.

'Get out of here as fast as you can,' the Doctor said, turning back from the doors. The passage was already empty apart from himself and Henry. 'Oh, they have. That's good.'

As the Doctor and Henry ran after everyone else, Gabby hurried up to them.

'What's going on?' Gabby asked. 'Why are the shareholders leaving the meeting? Where are Sir Manning and Miss Sark?' She brushed her long blonde hair away from one ear. She was wearing a large earring made from coloured glass twisted into a spiral. The shrieking from behind the doors grew louder.

Henry grabbed Gabby's arm. 'There's no time to explain now. We have to get away from here.'

The three of them set off down the corridor at a run. Gabby was still asking what was going on. From behind them, they all heard wood splinter and tear.

The Krillitanes were breaking through the doors.

'What about everyone else in the hotel?' Henry gasped as they reached the reception area. 'Shouldn't we warn them? Sound the fire alarm or something?'

'I don't think the Krillitanes will reveal themselves just yet. They want to keep everything secret, which is why they had to silence the shareholders.'

'Haven't you forced their hand? Or whatever they have instead of hands?'

'Will you two please tell me what's going on?' Gabby said. 'What was that noise? Why were the shareholders so scared? What's happened to Sir Manning and Miss Sark and the others?'

'In a minute,' the Doctor told her. He led the way out of the hotel and down a side street. 'I don't think they're chasing us, which is good. But I'm not sure that little adventure achieved as much as I'd hoped.'

'You found out their plan,' Henry said.

'Well, some of it,' the Doctor told him. 'But I'd like to know how advanced things are and what happens next.'

'You saved people's lives,' Henry insisted. 'They'd be dead now if we hadn't been there.'

The Doctor smiled. 'Yes. That's true, and that's the most crucial thing of all. Thank you, Henry.' He turned to Gabby. 'Now, it's time for some explanations.'

'At last,' Gabby said.

There was silence for a while.

Finally, Gabby said, 'Well, go on,

then—explain.'

'No, no,' the Doctor said. 'That's not what I meant.' He pushed his hands into his jacket pockets. 'Oh, that reminds me. I think this is yours.' He pulled something from his pocket. It was a small spiral of coloured glass.

'What is it?' Henry asked.

'Part of Gabby's earring.' The Doctor reached out and gently brushed Gabby's hair aside, to show her other earring was missing. 'See?'

Gabby took the piece of glass. 'Thank you, Doctor. Where did you find it?'

'It was clutched in poor Jeff's dead hand,' the Doctor told her, 'which is why I think it's time you gave us some explanations, Gabby.'

The air shimmered and blurred round Gabby. Her face seemed to go out of focus for a moment. Then it reformed, but in a new shape. It was the long, stony face of an angry Krillitane.

CHAPTER NINE

When the Krillitane spoke, its voice was Gabby's, only deeper and more gruff. 'Is this explanation enough for you, Doctor?'

'More of a good guess that's been confirmed.'

The Krillitane sniffed. 'You are not afraid of us. How strange. I can smell Henry's fear, but you are something different.'

'You're going to kill us,' Henry said, looking around. The side street led only to the back of the hotel. At the moment it was deserted, so no one would see what happened.

'Of course,' Gabby replied. 'Though in your case it will be no great loss.'

'Unfair!' the Doctor protested. 'You owe Henry a lot, and you know it.'

'Me? What do they owe me?'

Henry asked. 'I've done nothing for *them*.'

'Not on purpose,' the Doctor assured him. 'But I've seen the computer files. I've seen what your department does, as well as running the systems.'

'We needed a human,' Gabby growled. 'Someone to shield us from the day-to-day tasks and the tricky questions.'

'Me?'

'You, Henry,' the Doctor agreed. 'They used you right from the start. They used you to handle the health and safety inspectors, the VAT men, and any other officials who came snooping.'

'Why me? Why not someone else?'

'You were ideal,' Gabby said. 'You had no imagination to ask questions of your own. You were so bungling and lacking in skill that anyone could see there was no point asking anything difficult.'

'And of course,' the Doctor added,

'you didn't really know anything useful. The perfect front man. Or if it all went wrong, the perfect fall guy.'

Henry looked down at the ground. 'I always knew I was rubbish at my job,' he said, 'but I never guessed that was why I was given the job in the first place.'

'Humans are so stupid,' Gabby told him.

'No,' the Doctor said. 'No, I won't have that. You used Henry, you played on his character. But he's not stupid. You got him wrong. Humans are clever and imaginative. You just wait. Henry will show you.'

The Krillitane laughed. 'Henry will die. There is nothing clever about that.' Gabby drew herself up to her full height. Her claws glinted in the morning sun as she prepared to strike.

'She's right, Doctor.' Henry sounded defeated and tired. 'There's nothing clever about me. I have no imagination. We're going to die, right here and right now. Look,' he went on, pointing past the Krillitane towards the other end of the street. 'Here come the rest of her alien friends to gloat at us.'

Without thinking, Gabby the Krillitane turned to look where Henry was pointing, but the Doctor could see that the street was empty. There were no Krillitanes coming.

As soon as the creature turned, Henry leaped forward and shoved it hard in the back. The Krillitane staggered forwards, slipping off the kerb. It struggled to retain its balance.

That gave the Doctor and Henry time to run the other way down the street, towards the main road.

'Well done, Henry,' the Doctor said. 'Clever and imaginative. I knew you could do it.'

'We're not safe yet,' Henry pointed out. 'She'll be after us in a minute.'

They had reached the main road.

There was lots of traffic there. The morning rush hour was in full swing. The Doctor waved down a cab and they both got inside. The Doctor gave the address of the Brainy Crisps firm.

'Now they know we're on the loose, they'll bring the project forward,' the Doctor explained. 'They'll be using all the computer power they can. They'll want to finish as soon as possible, before we can cause trouble.'

'But that computer power is mostly on the internet,' Henry said.

The Doctor nodded. 'The more power they hijack, the less there will be to do other internet tasks. The whole system will start to collapse as the Krillitanes divert power to their own project.'

'And this project is building a creature, right? You said they were designing themselves again.'

'Yes, they are probably building a whole bunch of creatures to their new, improved design. The Krillitanes must have a facility somewhere with huge nutrient tanks where they grow the new creatures. The last stage will be to add intelligence and character, race memories and aggression.'

'Then we don't want to go to the office. There's nowhere there they could do all that.'

'So, where?' the Doctor wondered.

'The crisp factory,' Henry said, realising. 'There's a whole secret area at the Brainy Crisps factory where they research and develop new snacks.'

'New *snacks*?' the Doctor said. 'New *life*! Well done, Henry. I hope you know where this factory is.'

Henry gave the address of the factory to the cab driver. 'How long will it take?' he asked.

'No idea, I'm afraid.' The driver gave his sat-nav a thump. 'This thing's supposed to give me the latest traffic details, but it's gone crazy. It says Tower Bridge is staying open all day, and Oxford Street's closed because of a plague of locusts!'

'It gets the traffic news from the internet,' Henry told the Doctor. 'It's starting: the systems are breaking down.'

'I can get you there all right,' the driver assured them. 'I know the way. I just don't know what the traffic will be like.'

'The beginning of the end of the world,' the Doctor said, 'and I'm stuck in a traffic jam. Typical.'

'But we can stop the Krillitanes, can't we, Doctor?'

'They're no match for you and me, Henry. We can stop them, but only if we get there in time. We must prevent a new race of even more deadly Krillitanes from hatching. I have a nasty feeling that nothing will stop those creatures once they get out.'

CHAPTER TEN

The taxi dropped the Doctor and Henry at the gates to the crisp factory. It was a large building that looked like an aircraft hangar, but with tall chimneys at one end. The Doctor had his 'Access All Areas' badge. He and Henry showed their badges to the guard at the gate.

'Are you here for the meeting with all those bigwigs from the firm?' asked the guard.

'Probably,' the Doctor said. 'Tell me more.'

'Oh, just that you know something's going on when Sir Manning and Miss Sark and most of the rest of the firm's directors turn up with no warning.'

'And they headed for the research area, right?'

The guard said that this was indeed where they had gone. 'You'll need written consent from Sir Manning to get in there. They won't let you in without it.'

Henry looked worried, but the Doctor patted the pocket where he kept his psychic paper. 'No problem.'

'They got here before us,' Henry said as they walked up to the factory.

'They can fly. That solves the traffic problem.'

'Right. Yes. I still have a bit of a problem with this whole alien thing,' Henry said.

'You'll get used to it.'

They reached the door that Henry said led into the research area. It was locked, and there was no sign of a guard.

'There should be someone,' Henry said. 'At the main gate they said we needed Sir Manning's permission to get in.'

The Doctor agreed, and set to work with his sonic screwdriver. Soon he had the door open.

Once inside, they saw why there

was no guard. Half a dozen men in dark uniforms lay sprawled across the floor. From their wounds, the Doctor could tell they had been killed by the Krillitanes.

'They don't care any more,' the Doctor said sadly. 'The project must be even closer to completion than I thought.'

'But where are they?' Henry whispered.

The research area took up only a small part of the huge factory, but there were a few offices as well as the main workshop space. Massive metal tanks rose to the high ceiling. The Doctor tapped the side of one, and checked the displays on the pipes and tubes.

'It's full,' he told Henry. 'Nutrients and acids. The stuff of life. This is where it all happens—inside this tank.'

'Are we too late, then?'

'Oh no. The new Krillitane bodies must be nearly ready, but they will still need to program the creatures' brains. They need to load character and behaviour, the way the creatures think and how they act.' The Doctor grinned and explained his plan.

Henry led the way to one of the small offices, and turned on the computer. 'I don't know if I can get into the systems we need. This is the firm's internal website.' He pointed to the screen. 'It's already going haywire as the internet breaks down under the pressure of the Krillitane code. Look, the canteen menu says it's serving DNA with Custard for pudding today.'

The firm's online diaries were scrolling pages of Krillitane code. The Brainy_Crisps site didn't have the test any more. Now it showed the weather forecast for the Shetland Isles.

Finally, between them, they got access to the factory's own online systems. If it all worked, then Henry could control the whole output of the factory. He could change the amount of salt and oil in the crisps. He could get the systems to slice the potatoes thicker or thinner. He could even change the ingredients.

'Apple crisps might be nice,' the Doctor said. 'Or turnip. What do you think, turnip? Maybe not. Just do what you can,' the Doctor told Henry. 'I'm relying on you, Henry. The world is relying on you.'

'No pressure, then,' Henry muttered.

They both ducked down below the window as a shadow crossed it. A Krillitane was standing outside the office. They waited, then Henry breathed a long sigh of relief as the creature moved away at last. The Doctor let himself out of the room. He had another job to do.

*   *   *

The Doctor saw several Krillitanes as he crept through the factory. They were no longer in their human forms. That made them easier to spot, of course, but it was a worry that they were so confident.

A group of four of the creatures stood by one of the massive tanks. The Doctor guessed they were waiting for the process to finish. It probably wouldn't be long now. When all the Krillitanes were looking the other way, he ran to the next of the tanks.

One of the Krillitanes turned as the Doctor hurried past. Perhaps it caught sight of a blur of movement, a shadow moving across the floor. The Doctor took shelter behind the tank. It was an enormous steel drum.

The Doctor put his ear to the metal. Deep inside he could hear something moving. He could imagine the new breed of Krillitane creature thrashing in the liquids that gave it energy and life. The fluids that kept it fed and healthy as it grew.

He wondered what it would look

like. Would it be like the Krillitanes now patrolling the factory? Or would it be very different? He knew that, unless he acted now, he would soon find out.

The Doctor found the main control valve. This was what fed Krillitane Oil and other nutrients into the tanks. He pulled out his sonic screwdriver and aimed it at the valve.

A clawed hand clamped down on the Doctor's shoulder. It dug in, sharp and painful. Another claw knocked his sonic screwdriver aside.

The Krillitanes all looked very similar. But there was enough difference in their features and colour for the Doctor to recognise Sir Manning. Behind him, the Doctor could see Stella Sark and Gabby, watching him with hungry eyes.

'You really thought you could defeat us, Doctor?' Sir Manning said.

The Doctor pulled himself free of

the painful grasp. He rubbed at his shoulder and stretched. 'Careful, that hurt.'

'I'm so pleased.'

'Kill him,' Stella Sark said.

'Oh, don't I get to see the final product?' the Doctor complained. 'You said yourself, I can't defeat you now. Why don't you let me live a bit longer. At least then you can have a decent gloat. How did you find me, anyway?'

'We guessed you would come,' Gabby said.

'You see, Doctor,' Sir Manning added, 'you are so very predictable. In a few moments you will indeed witness our victory. Before you die.'

CHAPTER ELEVEN

'Well, I hope it's worth it all,' the Doctor said. 'I mean, hijacking the internet and making all those crisps.' He could see patches of dark, burned skin on Sir Manning and Miss Sark. 'I hope there's no lasting damage, by the way.'

Miss Sark hissed with anger. 'We should kill you now. Why wait?'

'Well, that's right,' the Doctor agreed. 'You're keeping me alive so I can witness your big success. Only, what if it isn't such a big success? What if it all turns out to be a bit rubbish? That would be such a waste of effort. Not to say embarrassing.'

The Krillitane that was Gabby stepped forward. Her claws clicked on the concrete floor, sending up sparks. 'Why did he come here?' she asked. 'What was his plan? He still seems very sure of himself. What can he have done?'

The Sir Manning Krillitane hurried over to the valves and pipes where the Doctor had been working.

'It seems we found you just in time. You were going to open the main flow valve from the oil feed,' he guessed.

'Oh, someone's getting clever. Been at those Brainy Crisps, have we?'

'If he had opened this main valve,' Sir Manning explained to the other Krillitanes, 'the oil would have gushed out of its tank. It would have spread through the whole place.'

'Highly inflammable cooking oil flooding the building.' The Doctor smiled. 'Sounds like a recipe for disaster, if you ask me.'

'You should show some respect,' Miss Sark snapped. 'Your only hope is gone. What is it they say? You win some, you lose some.'

'No,' the Doctor replied. 'Well, yes, they do say that. But it's not true. Not in my case. You see, I win them all.'

'It's over, Doctor,' Sir Manning said. 'You and your stupid friend . . .' His voice tailed off and the creature swung round. 'Where's Henry?' he demanded.

'Ah, sorry. He had to go home. Wasn't feeling too good.' The Doctor patted his pockets. 'I've got a sick note somewhere . . .'

'He's here,' Gabby realised. 'Henry is still hiding here in the factory.'

'Find him!' Sir Manning ordered.

Gabby hurried away, her wings beating urgently. Sir Manning turned back to the Doctor. 'Where is Henry? What is he doing?'

The Doctor sighed, and made a point of brushing dust off his lapel. 'You made the same mistake as Gabby.'

'What mistake is that?' Miss Sark asked.

'You undervalued Henry. Just like you've undervalued all the humans on this planet. You're going to pay for that. Unless you leave now.' The Doctor's eyes were hard, his face grave. 'I don't usually give another last chance. You don't know how lucky you are. Leave now, while you can.'

They did not laugh at the Doctor's words this time. Sir Manning turned his large head towards Miss Sark. 'Find Henry. Get all the brothers and sisters to search. We are so close, we cannot be denied our destiny now.'

*   *   *

Henry was feeling pleased with himself. He had at last managed to log into the factory systems. They were messed up by the problems with the internet, but he thought he could find a way to do what the Doctor wanted.

His biggest challenge was to stay safe. More than once, Krillitanes walked past the office and he had to duck down out of sight, but he was soon absorbed in his task.

In fact, he was so absorbed that he didn't notice the door swing open. A shadow fell across the desk.

'Be with you in a minute,' Henry said, out of habit. He was used to people waiting to talk to him while he worked in his office.

Except he wasn't in his office, he remembered. Nervously, Henry looked up.

A Krillitane was looming over him. With a snarl of rage, it reached over the top of the desk. It grabbed Henry's shoulders. He felt the claws pierce his jacket and his shirt. Then the Krillitane hauled him up from the chair.

Clamped hard against the creature's bony chest, Henry could not move. The creature snarled with glee, and dragged him away.

*   *   *

Sir Manning's alien eyes narrowed as he watched the Doctor. There were just the two of them now, standing between the giant metal tanks.

'You're too clever to be caught so easily,' said Sir Manning.

The Doctor grinned at him. 'You're so kind. But no, you caught me fair and square, so well done, you.'

'You came here on purpose. You knew that the most obvious action you could take against us would involve the oil.' Sir Manning looked up at one of the huge metal tanks beside them. 'There is enough Krillitane Oil in that tank to destroy this whole factory. Because of the way the process works, it has to be right next to the birth-tank. That is where the new Krillitanes are being created.' He turned to gesture at the tank on the other side of them. 'As I say, it was an obvious target.'

'There you are, then.'

'*Too* obvious. You were certain to

99

fail, and you knew that.'

'Perhaps I'm not as clever as you look.'

'Or perhaps that was not really your plan at all. You lured us here while Henry did the real work. Tell me, Doctor—what has he been doing? Where is he?'

The Doctor met Sir Manning's gaze. 'Henry will stop you. Be sure of it.'

There was a cackle of alien laughter from behind him. The Doctor spun round, and saw Krillitane Gabby drag Henry round from the other side of the tank.

'Not so clever after all,' she said. She pushed Henry away from her, and he stumbled and fell.

The Doctor helped Henry to his feet. 'Did you do it?' he whispered urgently.

Before Henry could answer, Sir Manning pulled the Doctor away.

'You see, Doctor, you simply cannot win. Your friend failed. In moments now the final data will finish flowing into the new Krillitanes. A race will be born. A new race of Krillitanes that will conquer the universe. We have won!'

From the huge metal drum that Sir Manning had called the birth-tank came a sound. It was a scraping, scratching sound. Then a muffled boom.

It was the sound of the creatures inside trying to get out.

CHAPTER TWELVE

Henry and the Doctor stood next to the birth-tank. Stella Sark checked the gauges and read-outs.

'It's almost complete,' she reported to Sir Manning. 'The last data is being programmed into the new Krillitane creatures even as we speak.'

'Then gather the brothers and sisters,' Sir Manning said. 'This is an historic moment. They should witness it.'

Miss Sark hurried away, her claws clicking on the concrete floor.

Sir Manning turned to the Doctor and Henry. 'You will witness it too. The final triumph of the Krillitanes. The beginning of a whole new race of creatures that will conquer all before them.'

The Doctor sighed. 'Yawn,' he said.

The tank containing the creatures shuddered under an impact from inside.

'How will they get out?' Henry wondered.

Sir Manning's alien features twisted into a smile. 'Oh, they'll find a way.'

The other Krillitanes arrived. There were about a dozen of them. They gathered round Sir Manning and Miss Sark. The Krillitane that had disguised himself as Clive gave a hiss of amusement when he saw the Doctor and Henry.

The sounds from inside the tank got louder. A dent appeared in the side of the tank, close to the Doctor and Henry.

'The creation fluids and liquids are being pumped out,' one of the Krillitanes reported.

'The process is complete,' another added. 'All personality and character details have been fed into the creatures.'

'Not just creatures,' Sir Manning said proudly. 'Krillitanes. *Super-Krillitanes.*'

Another dent appeared in the tank. The metal began to split. With a wrenching, tearing sound, a hole appeared. Massive claws reached out, ripping the metal aside like paper.

Henry watched in horror. The whole building echoed with the screeching sound of tearing metal.

'I'm not sure I like the look of that,' the Doctor said.

'Behold—our future!' exclaimed Sir Manning.

As he spoke, a whole section of the tank was forced aside. A massive creature stepped out. It stood, breathing deeply and looking around. Behind it two more of the huge creatures forced their way out of the tank.

They did not look very much like the other Krillitanes. These creatures were about three metres tall and deep red in colour. Their bodies were wet with the remains of the fluids from the tank. Their wings seemed more sleek and elegant.

Their faces were the most different. They were rounder, with less gaunt features. They looked almost human, like innocent children. Stubby horns stuck up from the tops of their heads, and they had long, sharp claws.

'They're like angels,' Henry gasped. 'OK, red angels. With horns and claws.'

'Angels,' the Doctor murmured. He looked at the original Krillitanes. 'And demons. But you're right, there is a family likeness.'

'They might look different, but they are so much stronger,' Miss Sark said.

'And far more clever,' Sir Manning added.

The Doctor sniffed. 'Well, that wouldn't be so hard, would it?'

Sir Manning's stony lips curled in

anger. 'For all their differences, they are still Krillitanes. You will be the first to witness their strength and power. Their ferocity, lack of mercy, and single-minded killer instincts.'

'And that all comes from their character programming?' the Doctor said. 'The last part of the data that you got from the puzzles and tests on the Brainy_Crisps website, yes?'

'Of course,' Miss Sark said.

'The website that Henry here has been in charge of.'

'Yes,' Sir Manning said. There was a hint of uncertainty in his voice now.

'And the personality and instinct all comes from the tests that cover intelligence and reason, don't they? And the ones that asked about war and anger? About fighting and hatred?'

'The best way to get the data we needed.'

'Yes, I thought so.' The Doctor stuffed his hands into his pockets.

There was silence for several

moments. Sir Manning and the other Krillitanes looked at each other confused. The three new Super-Krillitane creatures stood watching silently. Their eyes glinted as they caught the light.

'Is there some point you are trying to make, Doctor?' Sir Manning asked. 'Before you die, that is.'

The Doctor shrugged. 'Not really.' He turned to Henry. 'Anything you wanted to add?'

'Um . . .' Henry said. He sounded nervous. He glanced up at the glistening, red creature standing right beside him. The talons at the ends of its fingers were as long as Henry's own fingers. 'Not really,' he decided. 'Except that I guess the way these beasts behave is very much to do with what data was fed in. It depends on the results of the tests.'

'Of course,' Sir Manning said. 'And now we shall have one final test. We shall see how quickly our new brothers can rip you to shreds.' He looked up at the three massive creatures. 'The time has come, my brothers. Kill these two.' He pointed at the Doctor and Henry.

The three creatures turned towards the Doctor and Henry. One of the huge new Krillitanes reached out its clawed hand towards the Doctor. Henry and the Doctor backed away as the creatures advanced.

CHAPTER THIRTEEN

Henry looked scared, but the Doctor seemed completely at ease.

'This will be interesting,' the Doctor said loudly. 'Have you any idea what would happen if the wrong data got fed in? If, instead of all that hate and anger, the data came from a different website? Say, one where people talked about manners and how to be polite.'

'You mean, discussions about which cutlery to use at a dinner party, and how to talk to a bishop or the Queen?' Henry asked.

'That sort of thing,' the Doctor agreed.

The nearest of the Super-Krillitanes loomed over the Doctor.

'You talk such nonsense, Doctor,' Sir Manning said. 'That nonsense stops now. Kill him. Kill them both!'

The first of the huge creatures was

almost treading on the Doctor's toes. Fluid dripped from the tip of one of its talons, and splashed to the floor.

The Doctor reached out and grabbed the clawed hand that was coming towards him. With a huge grin, the Doctor shook the new Super-Krillitane's hand.

'So, how's it going, big fellow? I'm the Doctor, and this is my friend Henry.'

The Super-Krillitane's voice was a surprise. It was refined and cultured. 'Delighted to meet you both. I don't think we have names as such.' It turned its massive head towards the two other huge creatures. 'Do we?'

'I don't think we do,' one of the others agreed.

'Pretty sure we don't,' the third one said. 'Something we need to sort out.'

'Well, this is all a bit confusing and new, isn't it, Henry?' the Super-Krillitane said to Henry. 'If I may call you Henry?'

Henry nodded weakly.

'Thank you so much. Feeling a bit peckish, actually. You don't happen to have a cucumber sandwich or something of the sort about your person, do you?'

'Perhaps the Doctor and Henry will be free to come out and play later,' one of the other Super-Krillitanes said.

'That would be nice,' the Doctor said. 'Wouldn't that be nice, Henry?'

'Very nice,' Henry agreed.

The original Krillitanes watched this exchange with rising disbelief.

'What is going on?' Gabby asked.

'Something's wrong,' Miss Sark said coldly.

'Kill them!' Sir Manning shouted. 'Kill them now, you fools!'

The three new creatures looked at each other.

'We can't do that,' one of them said.

'They want to come out and play. You can't go round killing your

111

friends, you know.'

'What sort of society would that lead to?' asked the Super-Krillitane that had shaken the Doctor's hand. 'You're a bit strange, you are.'

Sir Manning was hopping from clawed foot to clawed foot. 'What have you done, Doctor?'

The Doctor smiled. 'I've done nothing. But Henry—you remember Henry, who you thought was a bit stupid? Well, he's not stupid at all, is he? Because he changed the data coming into your new Super-Krillitane brothers. Yes,' he said sounding pleased with himself, 'a great success, don't you think?' He caught sight of the Sir Manning Krillitane's angry face. 'Oh, you don't think so. That's a shame.'

'Shame,' echoed one of the new Super-Krillitanes.

Sir Manning and Miss Sark looked at each other. 'If you won't kill them,' Sir Manning said, 'then we will. Then we shall start this whole project again.'

'No, no, no,' the Doctor said. 'It's over. Can't you see that? Just put it down to experience and leave this planet.'

Sir Manning and the other original Krillitanes did not listen. They hurled themselves at the Doctor and Henry. Their wings flapped as they launched forwards, snarling in anger.

The three new Super-Krillitanes at once stepped in the way.

'You're not hurting our friends,' one of them said.

'We've only just met them,' another pointed out.

For a moment, the savage Krillitanes paused. Only for a moment, though. Then Miss Sark gave a cry of rage and leaped forward again.

'You are a disgrace to the name of Krillitane,' she shouted.

The nearest of the new Super-Krillitanes swatted her aside as if she were a fly. Miss Sark clanged into the side of a metal tank. At once she was up again, wings beating as she flew back towards the Super-Krillitanes.

The fight was becoming a battle between the two types of Krillitane. The Doctor and Henry watched as the smaller, more vicious original Krillitanes attacked the larger ones. A huge clawed foot stamped down, just missing Henry. Sparks flew from the claw as it cracked into the concrete floor. The Doctor pulled Henry back out of the way.

'This is not what we planned,' Sir Manning yelled. 'These vile creatures are not worthy of us. They must be destroyed.' He swept into the attack again.

It was all rather one-sided. The new creatures were larger, but didn't have the anger or savage nature of the original Krillitanes. Soon, one of the massive creatures was lying dead on the ground.

Sir Manning's group also had wounded and dead, but they drove the two larger creatures back. Several Krillitanes attacked one of the Super-Krillitanes at once. They flew into it, and knocked it flying backwards into one of the metal tanks. The creature tried to fight back, but it was overwhelmed.

In its dying moments, the enormous creature lashed out. Its claws missed Gabby, and ripped into the side of the metal tank. The sharp points punched holes in the tank. Dark liquid spurted out over the dying creature, soaking the other Krillitanes too.

At once they started to shriek. Their skin began to smoke and blister. Gabby screeched in sudden pain.

'Krillitane Oil,' Henry realised. 'That tank is full of it!'

The oil was pooling on the floor. It spread out across the concrete, running in rivers towards the Doctor and Henry.

It was running towards the other

Krillitanes too. The last of the massive new creatures seemed not to mind it, but the original Krillitanes backed away in fear.

Only Sir Manning and Miss Sark dared to attack again. They flew at the last Super-Krillitane, shrieking in anger. They drove the creature back with the force of their attack.

Finally, the huge Super-Krillitane fell. It collapsed to the floor like a tree being felled. For a moment it lay, staring across at the Doctor and Henry. Its mouth twisted into what might have been a sad smile.

'Sorry about all the trouble,' it said in a weak voice. 'I'd run for it if I were you.'

Sir Manning stood over the fallen body. 'Yes, run, Doctor. Run from the might of the Krillitanes.'

'Er, no, actually,' the dying creature said politely. Its voice was weak and frail, and it raised a massive clawed hand. 'I meant run from the fire.'

116

Miss Sark and Sir Manning were about to attack again. They froze, standing over the creature. Krillitane Oil from the leaking tank pooled round the dying Super-Krillitane.

'What fire?' Miss Sark said.

The large red Super-Krillitane gave a great sigh as it died. Its raised arm crashed down. Its claws hammered into the concrete floor, sending up a shower of sparks.

The Krillitane Oil caught fire at once. A wave of flame rolled across the floor, and Krillitanes exploded as it touched them.

The Krillitane that had been Clive managed to get high into the air, above the flames. Then the storage tank exploded in the heat, and Clive the Krillitane was engulfed in the fireball.

The Doctor and Henry ran, their arms over their heads to try to ward off the heat. Henry was choking on the black, smoky fumes.

'This way!' the Doctor yelled.

A dark shape reared up in front of them. Even in her Krillitane form, the Doctor could tell it was Gabby.

The fire rushed towards her. A wall of flame flared up between Gabby and the Doctor and Henry.

'Help me!' Krillitane Gabby shrieked. She backed away from the fire.

Henry started forwards, but the Doctor grabbed his arm.

'There's no way through. I'm sorry.' He raised his voice, so that Gabby could hear him through the fire. 'I'm so sorry.'

The Doctor walked quickly away.

Henry waited a moment, but there really was nothing he could do. He turned away, and followed the Doctor.

CHAPTER FOURTEEN

Together, Henry and the Doctor watched from the road nearby as the factory burned. Soon fire engines arrived, then an ambulance. The Doctor and Henry both knew they would find no one and nothing alive inside.

'Well done, Henry,' the Doctor said. 'They really did misjudge you.'

Henry shook his head. 'I never wanted this.' He pointed to the fire, which was still burning brightly.

'Nor did I,' the Doctor said. 'All that effort. They were so clever. So misguided. They actually created new life, a whole new race . . .' He shook his head sadly. 'Such a waste. Could have been worse though,' he decided.

'Really?'

'Oh yes. You and I could have been burned to a crisp.'

119

Henry laughed. 'I suppose so. I guess my job's gone up in smoke as well as the factory, though.'

'I guess so,' the Doctor agreed. 'Your pension's OK, though. I fixed that for you in the main computer.'

'I still need a job.' A thought occurred to Henry. 'You're not hiring, I suppose?'

The Doctor smiled sadly. 'Well, I do have a vacancy. I'm not looking for anyone to fill it just now, though, thanks all the same.'

'Pity.'

They walked slowly away down the road. Henry could feel the heat of the fire on his back.

'You'll think of something,' the Doctor said.

'I already have. I'm going to talk to James Purcell. He's a big shareholder in lots of other firms, and he knows about the Krillitanes. He saw them, after all. Maybe he can fix me up with something.'

'I'm sure he can,' the Doctor said.

120

'After all, you did save his life. Thanks for everything, Henry. You were brilliant. Just brilliant. If you need a reference, I'm your man.'

'Is the internet back to normal, do you think?' Henry asked.

The Doctor thought for a moment. 'I don't think you can really call the internet "normal", but yes—as close as it ever gets. Thanks to you, Henry. Thanks to you.'

*   *   *

It was a lovely sunny day. The last time the Doctor had walked along this street he was worrying about the internet. Now he knew it was fine. The strange virus the TARDIS had detected was the Krillitane code. Henry had sorted that out. He had closed the Brainy_Crisps website and shut down all the firm's computers. The Doctor had helped Henry delete all the alien code. All the crisps had been withdrawn from shops for

121

vague health and safety reasons.

The Doctor stood outside the TARDIS and looked round. Yes, it really was a lovely day, but it was time to be going. He had journeys to make, adventures to get on with.

He was about to unlock the TARDIS door, when a boy hurried past. The boy was about 12 years old and had untidy black hair. It was Spike, one of the boys that the Doctor had seen playing football. He was eating a bag of crisps.

The Doctor smiled as he remembered how the boy had explained to him about Einstein. 'Are those crisps any good?' the Doctor asked. 'How would you rate them on a scale of one to ten? Please take into account the taste value of each crisp and bear in mind the nasty effects of too much salt and fat. What do you think?'

The boy stared at the Doctor, his mouth open in surprise at the question. A crisp was half in and half out. The boy crunched up the crisp, still staring.

'Well?' the Doctor prompted.

In answer, the boy blew the loudest, longest raspberry the Doctor had heard for centuries. Then he laughed and ran off.

The Doctor grinned. Just as he had hoped, everything was back to normal. He unlocked the TARDIS and went inside.

A few moments later, the street was empty.